The Baby Flamingo
Who Wanted to Be Pink

Extraordinary Publishing

Amazon.com/author/extraordinary

Extraordinary Publishing

is dedicated
to publishing educational
picture books
and illustrated storybooks
to educate and inspire children.

Check out our author page for
more children's books:
Amazon.com/author/extraordinary

Far far away, on a large lake in East Africa, there lived hundreds of pink-feathered flamingos with very long legs.

Jack was a handsome flamingo
who was funny and friendly.

Jack was a care-free bachelor and spent a lot of time hanging out with his buddies.

One day, when Jack laid his eyes on Rose,
a beautiful female flamingo, he fell in love
with her at first sight.

Jack started courting Rose and brought her flowers to win her heart.

Jack invited Rose to a dance. They were both excellent flamenco dancers.

**Gradually, Rose fell in love with Jack.
And they were two flamingos in love.**

We're married!

**Jack wanted to spend the rest
of his life with Rose.
On a beautiful day,
Jack and Rose got married.**

**Very soon, their baby Lily was born.
Unlike her parents,
Lily had gray down feathers.**

I want to be pink!

Lily asked Rose,
"Mom, why am I gray?
I don't like being gray.
Why am I not pink
and beautiful like you?"

"Look at my cousins! They are all pink, beautiful and cool. Why am I gray?"

"Honey, all colors are beautiful.
You're beautiful the way you are.
I was also gray when I was born. When you
turn 3 years old, you will have pink feathers
like mom and dad. I love you no matter
you are gray or pink,"
Rose explained patiently.

Eat and grow pink!

Rose told Lily, "The pink color
of our feathers
comes from the food we eat.
If you want to be pink,
you must eat your food."
Rose fed Lily milk with her mouth.
Hearing this, Lily drank as much
milk as she could.

Rose's pink color started to fade
as she fed her daughter milk.

"Mom, what happened to you?"
Lily asked with concern.
"You're losing your color!"
"Don't worry. When you are old enough
to eat solid food, I can stop feeding you
milk and my color will come back," said Rose.

Rose asked Lily, "Now that I am less pink , do you still think I am beautiful?"
"Of course, you're beautiful. All colors are beautiful. I love you no matter what color you are. You're my superhero.
Mom, I love you so much," said Lily.

We're orange!

Rose told Lily, "By the way, honey,
not all flamingos are pink.
Some flamingos are orange."

"Other flamingos have black feathers
on their wings.
All colors are beautiful," said Rose.

**Lily loved wearing high-heeled shoes,
because she wanted to
be as tall as her mom.
"There's no hurry in becoming tall.
Enjoy being a kid. You may be taller than
me when you grow up," said Rose.**

**Rose gave Lily a pair of comfortable
dancing shoes.
Lily took to dancing immediately.**

**Lily dreamed of becoming a tall princess
and dancing like a ballerina.
All that dancing did help her grow faster.**

It's story time!

Rose read bedtime stories to Lily every night. She often told Lily that, "Reading makes you smart. Smart is the new beautiful."

Jack, Lily's father, got up early every day
to look for food for the family.
They loved eating shrimps and algae,
which gave them the pink color.

**At the end of the day, Jack brought
home delicious food for Lily and Rose.
Jack loved Lily and always fed
her patiently.
Jack was a good father.**

**On her third birthday, Lily turned pink.
"Hooray! I am pink now," exclaimed Lily.**

**By age 3, Lily was pink and beautiful,
just like her mom.
Thanks to her parents, she was
also smart and confident.**

A happy family of pink flamingos.

Made in the USA
Coppell, TX
08 July 2023

18893754R00019